My grace is all you need.
2 Corinthians 12:9

To Matt – from Mrs. Watkins
4·26·09

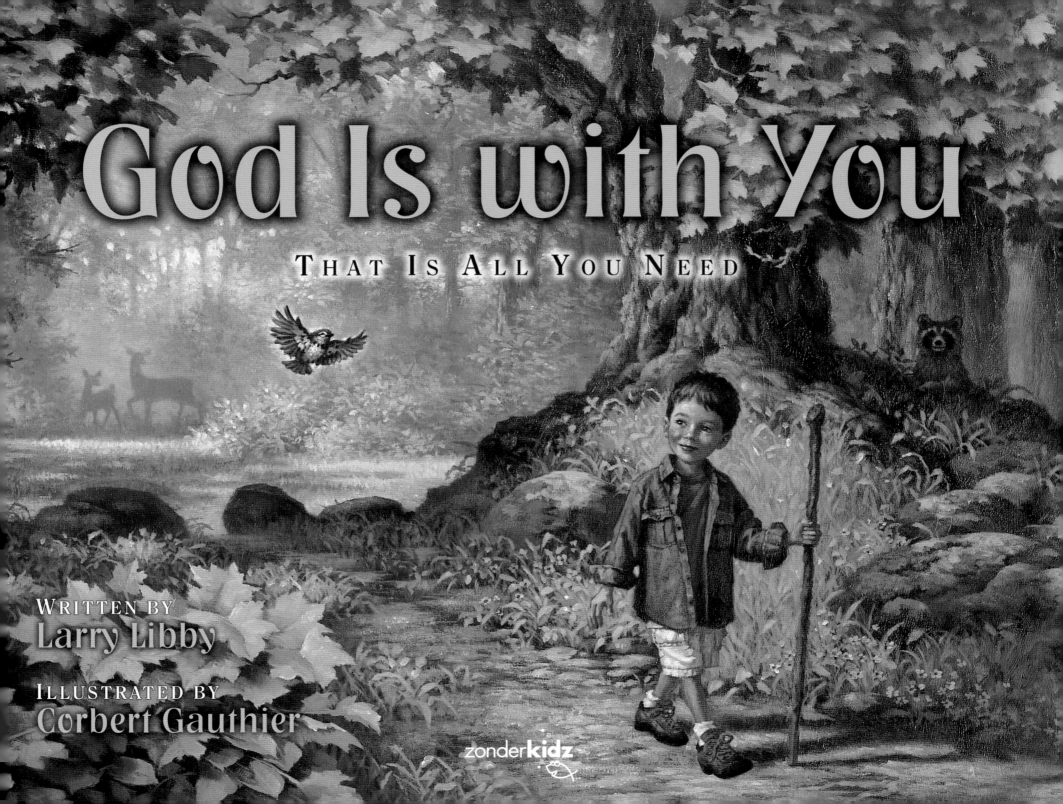

zonderkidz
The children's group
of Zondervan

www.zonderkidz.com

Editor: Gwen Ellis
Interior Design: Jody Langley
Art Direction: Laura Maitner

Printed in China
05 06 07 08 /CTC/ 7 6 5

In memory of my wife,
Laura Libby
now in Heaven
and with the Lord forever.

Larry Libby

For my very talented and helpful models.

Thanks to: Paddy, Jack, Megan, Hannah, Colerina, Danny, Andy, Aimee, Philip, and Lincoln (our dog).

Corbert Gauthier

When You're Facing a Scary Time, Remember God Is with You!

Everyone gets scared sometimes. Isaac was a man in the Bible who got scared. He moved his family to a new place, where the neighbors were unfriendly. But he had a good and loyal Friend he had almost forgotten about—God! The LORD appeared to him and said, *I am the God of your father Abraham. Do not be afraid. I am with you. I will bless you* (Genesis 26:24).

Did you hear what God said? "I AM WITH YOU!"

One time I went jogging after school with my friend Steve. We decided to run through the school, but when we got in, we couldn't get out. The door was locked.

At first it was funny, but then we started to get scared. We yelled and pounded on the windows. Our imaginations ran wild. What if we died of hunger? What if our parents called the police? What if...? Then we had an idea—a very bad idea. We picked up a heavy wooden planter full of flowers and hurled it through a window. *Crash!*

Just then the janitor came around the corner. He unlocked the door and let us out. If we had waited just a few more seconds, we would not have broken the window. We forgot that God is always with us.

The God who was Isaac's Friend in scary times is your Friend too. God would like us to remember him when we feel afraid.

When You Feel He Is Far Away, Remember God Is with You!

God is with you. That sounds nice, but isn't he sitting on a throne somewhere, while we live in plain old houses in plain old neighborhoods here on Earth? Don't worry. Jesus said, *I will ask the Father. And he will give you another Friend to help you and to be with you forever. The Friend is the Spirit of truth....He lives with you, and he will be in you* (John 14:16–17).

The special Friend Jesus promised is the Holy Spirit of God. He is with me, and he is in me forever. That means that somehow God the almighty Creator and King of Kings lives inside ME!

He couldn't be much closer, could he?

He's as close as my skin.

He's as close as my thoughts.

He's as close as my next breath.

He's as close as the beat of my heart.

And he is with me here RIGHT NOW!

When Everything Seems to Go Wrong, Remember God Is with You!

I remember a Little League baseball team where none of the boys had enough money to buy uniforms. The team decided to sell candy door-to-door to raise money. One boy, Maynard, sold more candy than anyone else. In fact, he was so busy selling candy, he didn't have time to practice baseball. On the day of the first game, Maynard's team looked sharp in their new white hats, purple jerseys, and flashy baseball pants. Maynard was so excited. He felt like a real baseball player!

When the game began, the other team came up to bat first, and Maynard, out in center field, felt sure he was ready. He was pretty sure that no one could hit the ball that far anyway. But right off the bat, someone smacked the ball right to him.

Maynard yelled, "I got it! I got it!" and stuck his glove high in the air. But he couldn't see where the ball was. He dropped his glove just for a moment and crack! The ball banged him right on the top of his head. Maynard screamed and threw down his glove. Then, he grabbed his head and ran home, crying all the way. Maynard quit the team after the very first pitch of the very first game.

That was too soon to quit. Have you ever felt like quitting? Don't be like Maynard and quit too soon. Remember that Jesus is with you to help you. When Jesus is in our lives, nothing is ever hopeless. The Bible tells us: *We have put our hope in him* (1 Timothy 1:1).

When You Have Hurts that Won't Go Away, Remember God Is with You!

Let's pretend that you've hurt your foot and can't walk. Now let's pretend that you have your very own angel to carry you around on his wide, strong shoulders. Wow! Wouldn't that be neat? Your angel would come to your bedroom early every morning and say, "Get up, sleepyhead. We've got places to go today." And then you'd get up, and the two of you would take off for great adventures.

Would you still be sorry that you had a hurt foot and couldn't walk? Sure you would, but it wouldn't be so bad if your very own angel were there to take you places.

I know something even *better* than having your own private angel. The Lord Jesus has promised to be with you *always*—right up to the end of the world. He is a better, more powerful, more wonderful Friend than a million angels.

It's no fun to get hurt, but most hurts do stop after a while. Just remember, the Lord Jesus is with you in:

> your old hurts and your new hurts,
>
> your big hurts and your little hurts,
>
> the hurts others know about, and . . .
>
> the hurts only you and God know about.

When People Tell Lies about You,
Remember God Is with You!

One day Mr. Lofton, my sixth-grade teacher, asked me to come out in the hall to talk. Mr. Lofton looked angry. I felt afraid. I had never been in trouble in his class before. He was holding a library book. When he opened it, I couldn't believe my eyes. Someone had drawn a bad picture on one of the pages. At the bottom it said, "By Larry Libby." It even looked like my handwriting. But I hadn't done it! It was a lie!

Have you ever had someone tell a lie about you? It hurts. But it's good to remember that God knows your heart. He knows the truth, and he will always stand beside you. And that's better than having the whole world stand beside you.

Jesus told his disciples, *I am the way and the truth and the life* (John 14:6). You see truth is not only something true, truth is also a person—named Jesus.

When the shining, radiant, wonderful, true Son of God is with you, the lies will soon fade away. I know, because the Lord was with me when I told Mr. Lofton the truth about the picture and he believed me.

When You Don't Know What's Ahead, Remember God Is with You!

I love to go places that I've never been before. Don't you? That's kind of the way it is with our lives. We are all going someplace we have never been before. Nobody knows what's going to happen next. The phone rings. Who is it? You don't know, do you? There is a knock on the door. Who is it? You don't know, do you? You open your mailbox. What is in there? You don't know, do you?

The only person who knows everything about tomorrow is God. How does God know? He's already been everywhere we are going. God can see tomorrow as well as he can see today and yesterday. Just think of that! He knows what's going to happen before the phone rings or the door opens or the mail comes.

God wants us to trust him each new day, no matter where we are going. When we worry or try to make things happen, we are not trusting him. Jesus said, *Don't worry about tomorrow. Tomorrow will worry about itself* (Matthew 6:34).

God has already been to all of your tomorrows, and he knows just what you'll need. More than that, he'll be there to help you every step of the way.

When It Seems Like Nobody Understands, Remember God Is with You

Do you have a favorite room? Can you close your eyes and, without peeking, remember where everything is in that room? I remember my grandparents' old white house that way. I can close my eyes and hear the old oil stove click-click-clicking as it heated up in the morning. I can see the old swivel chair sitting in front of the two big windows with a view of the fishpond and the apple orchard. I can see the closet where my grandparents kept the toys: a red plastic shaver that really buzzed and a jigsaw puzzle of an old mill. I loved that place. The house is an old wreck now with sad, empty windows and grass growing up through the front porch. But, in my imagination, I see it the way it used to be.

Just like I see the old house when it was at its best, so God sees the best in us. He loves us and he knows us. He knows the way we hold our mouths when we're puzzled about something. He knows our favorite color. He's looked into every one of our hiding places. He feels our disappointments, and he keeps our secrets.

Other people may not understand us at all. In fact, we may not understand ourselves very well. But God understands us. He made us. Remember? And nobody loves us more than he does.

When You're Feeling Sad and All Alone, Remember God Is with You!

One time after I was grown up, I went with some other Christians to a faraway country called Romania. I wanted to help some people who had physical problems. On the way, our plane stopped in Switzerland. A group of Christians came to welcome us. We sang and laughed and talked as if we were old friends. In the group was a sweet, young woman who had been born with no hands. But it didn't seem to matter. She had such a nice smile that people forgot she didn't have any hands.

When it was time to get back on the plane—there weren't enough seats! I was asked to stay behind and wait for another plane to come. I felt so alone as I watched my friends get on the plane without me. But the lady with no hands smiled at me and said, "Don't worry, Larry. You can stay at our house. You won't be alone." I felt so much better. But just as we were leaving, I heard my name over the loudspeaker. There was one seat left on the flight to Romania after all. And the plane was waiting for me.

As I ran to get on the plane, I turned and saw my friend with no hands waving with her arms. I may never see her again until we get to heaven. I am very glad that God sent someone so sweet to be with me when I was alone.

When you're alone, don't worry. God will always be with us, and he will often send someone to be with us. He is a Father who never leaves his children alone.

When You Think about This World Ending, Remember God Is with You

Have you ever thought about the end of the world? The Bible says that just as the world had a beginning, it will also have an end. God's going to roll up the old creation just like your mom rolls up dirty sheets on laundry day. Then when God shakes creation out again, everything will be new and fresh and clean.

There will be a new world with new galaxies, new stars, and new planets.

There will be a new Earth with new forests and mountains and valleys.

There will be a new you in a new strong body.

Does knowing this old world will end someday scare you? Sure, it's a scary thought because we really don't understand how it will happen. But King David wrote something in the Old Testament that can help us. He said,

God is our place of safety. He gives us strength.

He is always there to help us in times of trouble.

The earth may fall apart.

The mountains may fall into the middle of the sea.

But we will not be afraid …

The LORD who rules over all is with us.

Psalm 46:1, 7

Wow! The Lord who rules over everything is with us. He will bring us right out of the old world and into the new one—just like that!

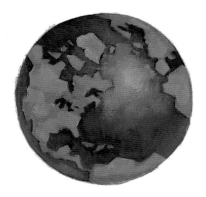

When the Path before You Is Dark and Dangerous, Remember God Is with You!

One Saturday morning, some kids met with their teacher, to hike to a place called Blue Pool where a swift, powerful river thunders down into a deep, blue, crystal-clear pool. The group was supposed to leave early, but some of the kids got there late. By the time they got started, it was already afternoon. The hike wasn't very long, but the kids walked slowly and took too long to eat lunch. When they got to Blue Pool, the sun was setting. Soon, it was very dark.

The kids were frightened. For one thing, the trail had steep, narrow places, and they couldn't see very well at all. Their teacher knew God was with them. "Let's pray," he told the little group. "Lord," he said, "it's awfully dark and we're afraid, but we know you are with us. Please help us find our way back to the car. In Jesus' name, amen."

The Lord heard their prayer. He gave the teacher the idea of having each person grab hold of the hand of the person in front of him. Together they walked safely down the trail, singing all the way.

If you ever find yourself in the dark, don't be afraid. Jesus is always with you, and he will show you the way. Jesus said, *"I am the light of the world"* (John 8:12).

When You Say Good-bye to Someone You Love, Remember God Is with You!

Have you ever been to a family gathering, maybe at Thanksgiving or Christmastime? If you have the kind of family that likes to get together, you know there are lots of hugs and laughs and yummy food.

Someday there is going to be the biggest family get-together of all—right in the middle of the sky! It's true. This is what the Bible says about it: *The Lord himself will come down from heaven. We will hear a loud command. We will hear the voice of the leader of the angels. We will hear a blast from God's trumpet. Many who believe in Christ will have died already. They will rise first. After that, we who are still alive and are left will be caught up together with them. We will be taken up in the clouds. We will meet the Lord in the air. And we will be with him forever* (1 Thessalonians 4:16-17).

That will be the best get together ever. Has someone you love gone to be with Jesus in heaven? All those people you've had to say good-bye to here on earth will be there. And Jesus will be there too. He will see you first! Your eyes will meet his eyes, and his arms around you will feel better than anything you've ever felt. And there will never have to be another reunion because you will be with those you love forever.

When You're Asked to Do Something Very, Very Hard, Remember God Is with You!

Peter was a fisherman, who lived near the Sea of Galilee. He knew how to handle his fishing boat very well, even at night. But one night, he and some of his friends were out fishing when a storm began to blow the boat every which way. Big waves pounded over them, and the wind whipped the sail. Peter and the others were very scared. They were friends of Jesus, but he wasn't in the boat with them that night.

Then suddenly, the men saw Jesus. He was standing on the churning sea and reaching out his hand to them. Jesus called out to Peter. "Come," he said. Jesus wanted Peter to climb out of the boat and walk to him on the water—without a life jacket or a scuba tank or anything. So Peter got out of the boat and started to walk to Jesus. At first he was all right, but then he looked at the waves. He became afraid and began to sink into the water. He cried out, "Lord! Save me!" Jesus pulled him up and helped him get back into the boat.

Has the Lord ever asked you to do something you thought you couldn't do? What if Jesus asked you to tell one of the kids in your class about him? You might say, "That's way too hard for me!" But if Jesus asks you to do it, he will help you—just like he helped Peter. That's all there is to it.

When Your Best Friend Moves Away,
Remember God Is with You!

Having a friend who loves Jesus as much as you do is just about the best thing in the whole world. Do you know why? It's because Jesus is holding both of your hands at the same time. And he will never let go of either one of you.

I know a little girl who had a club with her best friend. The two girls called their club The Christian Kindness Club or TCKC for short. One of their favorite places to meet was in our birch tree. They would hang out a club sign, climb the tree, and sit there chattering like birds. They had lots of fun together. Then one gray, rainy day, one of the girls and her family had to move far away. These days the girls write letters and send each other little gifts, but TCKC doesn't meet anymore.

Does that mean TCKC is gone forever? Probably not. Someday those two girls who shared so much love for Jesus and for each other will be together in heaven. There will be wonderful meetings of The Christian Kindness Club. I think maybe Jesus himself will be a member of that club. And no matter how busy he may be, he will never miss a meeting. Friends in Jesus are friends forever.

Someone at the Door

When your best friend wants to be with you, what does he or she do? I know what my best friend Steve would do. He would come flying up our front steps two at a time and knock on our door.

"That's Steve," I'd say before I opened the door. And I would be right.

But what if one day, I heard Steve's familiar knock on my door and decided not to open it? I wouldn't be much of a friend, would I?

Did you know that Jesus Christ, the mighty Son of God, has been knocking on the door of your heart? Did you know that he has been waiting for you to invite him into your heart? This is what he says in the Bible. *Here I am! I stand at the door and knock. If any of you hears my voice and opens the door, I will come in and eat with you* (Revelation 3:20).

Now maybe you've already invited him in. I hope so. But if you haven't, guess what? He is still knocking, and he still wants to come in. Turn the page and find out how to ask him into your life.

You Can Invite Jesus into Your Life
by Saying a Prayer Like this One.

Dear Lord Jesus,

Thank you for knocking on the door of my heart. Thank you for dying on the cross for all the bad, hurtful things I've done. I need to be saved from my sins. I want you to be Lord and King of my life. Please come into my life and be with me always. Amen.

Did you pray that prayer? Then always remember, wherever you are, whatever you are doing, you will always have someone with you and that Someone is God.